Fic

Written by The Cobbydale Quills

Book copyright © 2020 by David Driver
Book cover and art copyright © 2020 by David Driver
Second edition
Published by The Gingerlicious Company
Editing and formatting, Arthur G Mustard
Final edit and proofread, Colin Neville

All rights reserved. No part of this publication may be reproduced, stored in or introduced into a retrieval system, or transmitted, in any form, or by any means (electronic, mechanical, photocopying, recording or otherwise) without prior written permission of. This book is purely fiction. Names, characters, places and incidents are all the work of the authors` imagination or used fictitiously. Any resemblance to actual people living or dead, events or locales is coincidental.

All individual stories remain the copyright of the authors.

Foreword

'Winter Tales' was my first project which brought together a great mixture of writers. I asked the writers to include two of the following within their stories; winter, magic, good versus evil, adventure, Christmas or folklore. We also looked at the use of key words and three of these had to be included within their word weaving. Then came the curve ball: an unusual object from the table, and this also had to be part of the story. Discussions took place with regard to narrative, dialogue, openings and endings and we also 'shot off' on tangents when discussing chocolate, James Bond, Bill Sykes, Fagin, dislikes and many other non-related subjects. But in the end we all agreed that chocolate was indeed a good force for writing. Hopefully, we have all done as asked and these 'asks' reflect in the individual stories.

I have thoroughly enjoyed the project and loved working alongside a group of wonderfully talented and creative people. It has been a creative journey and I have learnt a little more about all of them and myself.

We shared not only our work, but many cups of coffee, tea, biscuits and chocolate. Many laughs were had along the journey and we also got to know each other a little better. The book has a mix of genres, with themes of mystery, fantasy, horror and stories for the young at heart. I would like to point out, that some of the stories may not be suitable for younger readers. So here is our first anthology.

I hope you enjoy the stories as much as we do.

Thank you

David

Cobbydale Quills

The Cobbydale Quills is a writing group based in Silsden, West Yorkshire, UK. The aim of the group is to bring writers together of all abilities, cultures, writing styles and all such like to work on a multitude of on-going projects.

Contributing authors

Marian Barker

Helen Bradley

David Driver

Faye Kelk

Wendy Kelk

Linda Tugwell

All of the above mentioned are wonderfully creative writers.

A special mention to Colin Neville and his beady eye.

Contents

A Fireside Tale by Marian Barker, page 7

The Stranger and the Ring by Helen Bradley, page 10

QA Greenbaum by David Driver, page 15

The Robin`s Christmas Adventure by Wendy Kelk, page 20

A Winter`s Tale by Linda Tugwell, page 25

Storm by David Driver, page 28

Jamie and The Gingerbread Man by Marian Barker, page 32

Mistletoe and Whine by Faye Kelk, page 35

The Doll by Linda Tugwell, page 41

Winter Tales

A Fireside Tale

*L*ong, long ago and very far away in the magical, mystical land of Oklothan was a small village called Iggonan. The village nestled in a valley between two mountains known locally as 'The Giant's Elbows'. Legend had it that Giants once roamed the country, striking terror amongst the Oklothians.

On cold winter evenings, the inhabitants of Iggonan would sit around their fireplaces and retell the many tales that had been passed from generation to generation. Nothing was written down and, as time went by, the stories became more and more exaggerated.

One particularly bitterly cold winter's evening, when a vicious storm was rampaging through the village, two young brothers were enjoying the warmth of the open fire. They were listening to their grandfather Olaf telling one of his many stories. The young boys huddled together whilst Olaf told them about the time when giants ruled the country. The old man loved to see the expressions on Josef's and Erik's faces as he told his tales. He clearly remembered how he listened to his own grandfather.

As always, the story began "Once upon a time, many, many years ago…."
Olaf continued.

"There were twin giants called Grindl and Borak. Twins were very rare amongst giants so everyone for miles around had heard about them. Grindl and Borak were strikingly different as they had dark curly hair. All the other giants had blonde straight hair.

From a very early age, the twins enjoyed the fact that they were different from the other children and liked being the centre of attention. Grindl was the taller of the two boys and by far the strongest of the pair. Borak was a survivor who idolized his brother and blindly followed him. Grindl loved being in charge and didn't take kindly to anyone who dared to disagree with him.

The brothers attended the local school and whilst Borak was a perfect student, Grindl was quickly turning into the school bully. Borak was embarrassed by his brother, but afraid to say anything to him. Meanwhile, Grindl was enjoying his notorious reputation. Their parents were not aware that anything was wrong and so the situation went unchecked.

As time passed by, Grindl became more and more unlikeable and the rest of the giants started to ignore him. Borak didn't know what to do because, deep down, he loved his twin. As he could no longer bully the other giants, Grindl turned his attention on the villagers in the nearby village of Iggonan and he began to terrorise them. He even scared the animals. The hens stopped laying eggs and cows no longer gave milk.

The villagers were distressed and frustrated. Grindl used to sleep all day, but his loud snoring echoed down the valley and filled the narrow streets with so much noise that everyone had to shout at each other to make themselves heard. The once quiet village had become an awful place to live.

By night things were just as bad, if not worse, as Grindl put on his hobnail boots and stomped all over the cobbled streets. He loved to tower above the tiny houses, flare his nostrils and breathe gusts of cold air down chimneys. His favourite sport was to tap on bedroom windows and wake the occupants and then quickly hide. The villagers grew very tired and very weary.

Borak didn't like his brother's behaviour and decided to try and help the inhabitants of Iggonan. Just before each dawn he would tiptoe into the village. He left jugs of milk and baskets of eggs outside the local inn before creeping back to his mountain home.

Grindl wasn't aware of his brother's kindness to the villagers so he was puzzled when they started to become more and more cheerful. They took to singing in the streets and the local band played loudly every afternoon. Grindl wasn't happy as the laughter and music drifted up the valley and filled the mountain air. This soon put a stop to the giant's daytime sleeping, but after a while he realised how relaxed and soothed he'd become. He still snored loudly every night, but the villagers started to find the noise quite comforting.

Grindl realised what an awful giant he'd become and was keen to make amends. News of Grindl's change of heart soon spread throughout the giant community. Once more, he found himself the centre of attention - but for all the right reasons.

Borak was happy to see the difference in his brother, but never once told him how he'd been instrumental in the transformation. Borak simply smiled and rested on his giant elbows.

The villagers no longer lived in fear of giants and their lives became richer. The village prospered and people came from miles around to listen to the band led by its new musical director called Grindl.

Erik and Josef laughed and clapped their hands.

"Tell us another story," Josef cried.

"Tell us about the snowflake and the silver compass," Erik added

Olaf shook his head and said that it was far too late, but he promised to tell them another of his tales the very next day.

The Stranger and the Ring

*D*anny finally moved. He stretched out his long legs towards the last licks of flame and rubbed large hands over a tired, grizzled face.

After sitting for so long he stood slowly, aching limbs creeping gradually back to life. The crockery from his scrappy dinner was scattered at his feet and he kicked it savagely out of the way, as he threw the remains of his umpteenth beer on the embers. The air sizzled and smoked, large grey trails vanishing up the black hole of the chimney.

A bit like my future, he thought grimly.

The house around him creaked and groaned more loudly than usual. It seemed to be crying along with Danny, who discovered wet drops on his cheeks. Erin would be in London by now, with Bill - Danny's ex best-friend.

Danny stood there, motionless, the enormity of Erin's betrayal becoming a real thing, growing inside him like a fatal disease, choking him like the acrid smoke from the dead fire.

He hurled his empty glass into the fireplace. Above, on the mantelpiece, lovingly placed by Erin's then faithful hands, were ornaments and memorabilia of their relationship. Danny swiped them away in one clear movement. They tumbled and crashed to the stone slab floor, scattering and splintering into pieces.

Through blurred eyes - whether tears or fury he couldn't tell - he saw the remains of the clock they'd picked out together. Erin had dragged him a mile and a half back to a shop they'd passed, when visiting Edinburgh.

"There!" she'd pointed excitedly at a purple clock, depicting a dragon like rose.

"That's hideous!" he'd replied, but she looked at him with the brown lakes of her eyes, pleading, and so the clock came home with them. It now lay in three bits, permanently frozen at ten past eleven, the hands bent and broken out of shape, as if pointing towards the uncertain future.

He picked up a photo of them both, also taken in Edinburgh; she blonde and pixie- like, with hair, as ever, sleek around her pointed chin; he gangly and black-haired, giraffe- like limbs, and a goofy grin. The frame had been hewn out of one large piece of rock, like something from the Flintstones; another of Erin's choices.

He threw it down again, crunched over the rest of the debris and dropped onto the sofa, suddenly overtaken by misery and his all-day long drinking session. Savagely, he pulled his wedding ring from his finger, launched it across the room and flopped back, soon falling into a blank sleep. He lay eight hours in the cooling house, which mourned around him, and then woke, cold and hung-over.

Danny groaned and once again coaxed his body back to life, easing himself up and heading towards the kitchen. Strong, black coffee and some burnt toast brought him physically round. Mentally he was a wreck.

He sat with his head in his hands, realising after some moments that he could not feel the cool, familiar hardness of his ring against his cheek. He remembered throwing it the evening before and began hunting where it should have landed, but couldn't find it. After searching for hours, the daylight had faded when he finally gave up.

Sitting on the floor, not able to energise himself to light a fire or even wash, he rubbed the groove in his finger left by the absent ring. He stared at nothing, feeling his marriage slipping further away. Then, slowly, he became aware of a loud knocking.

"Erin!" he shouted and jumped up, forgetting that she would have a key. He leapt to the door and flung it open excitedly.

A smallish man, dressed in beige clothes, with drab brown hair and too big glasses stood, there stamping his feet and jumping slightly. Bewildered and disappointed, Danny looked curiously at the snowflakes circling around the man and realised the weather had changed as much as his life in the last couple of days.

"Really sorry to bother you, but my car has broken down and it's stuck in the snow, just up there."

The man pointed in the direction of the road, which was invisible in the white shrouded darkness.

"And my mobile's dead of course! They always are when you need them most, aren't they?"

"Hnn", said Danny, non-committed.

"So, do you think I could borrow yours, and if at all possible, come in until the rescue people arrive?" The man looked at him hopefully through his spectacles, his eyes large with black centres.

Danny glanced around him, in vain hope that another solution would pop up from the snow. But there was none, so he held the door wide and the man passed him, bringing in a cloud of cold air and a lot of "Thank you... that's great ... life saver" comments.

"Cuppa?" Danny asked, begrudgingly, as he handed over his phone.

As the man fussed with finding the number to call, from a scrap of paper in his wallet, he nodded and smiled.

"Oh yes please, coffee, white with one. That would be a treat. My name is Michael by the way." He held out his free hand.

"Danny."

They shook hands briefly and Danny wandered out into the kitchen. He could hear talking, then a raised voice and the sounds of someone not getting what they want. He came back with a steaming mug just in time to hear Michael say, "Great, thanks for not very much!"

He hung up and gave Danny back his phone, taking the coffee.

"They can't come for three hours! I was supposed to be going to a friend's house for dinner. Guess it'll be a McDonald's on the way back home on the back of a tow truck!"

Danny ignored the hint and flopped on to his sofa, indicating that Michael could do the same.

"Well, you can wait here." He muttered ungraciously, as Michael divested himself of his coat and sat down.

"Listen, it`s none of my business," Michael began, "But are you OK, you look a little rough?"

Danny barked a sharp laugh, "Oh yeah I'm just dandy! Wife left, hung-over, stranger bothering me. I'm just tip- top."

Michael looked uncomfortable and stood up again.

"Hey, I'm sorry, don't want to be any trouble. You sound like you've got enough of that already."

Sighing, Danny pushed himself back to his feet, "No, I'm sorry. Not your fault. Tell you what, shall I make us some food? Pizza ok? It's all I've got though, so it will have to be."

Michael sat down again, and nodded his thanks as Danny once again lumbered out to the kitchen. A few minutes went by as Danny rustled in the freezer and switched on the oven. He turned around to find Michael standing in the doorway and jumped.

"Hell!" he said, "Can't you give some warning? I didn't hear you!"

"Just wondered what this is?" Unperturbed, Michael held up a small object, unperturbed. Danny peered at it then realised it was his wedding ring. "Just found it on the floor in front of the fire. Is it yours?"

Growling under his breath, Danny grabbed it and shoved it back on his finger.

"Yes, I dropped it. Thanks."

After an awkward pause he asked suddenly, 'Wait. Where was it?"

Michael led the way back into the living room and pointed at where he'd found it, at the complete opposite side of the room to where Danny had lobbed it the previous evening.

"Weird," he said.

"So, hate to pry, but when did she leave?"

"Yesterday morning," Danny said reluctantly, "With my best mate, just to add the extra touch!"

"God, I'm sorry, that's rough."

Michael stared at the floor for a moment then seemed to make a decision.

"You know, I'm not just a stranger with car trouble. I actually have an erm...gift...so to speak."

"Hnn?" said Danny again, that one syllable being his most useful at the moment.

"I think I can help you, with the situation with your wife, I mean."

Danny laughed, "God this is corny! Dark night, weird stranger turns up at my door and offers to do voodoo or whatever! No offence, but am I on Candid Camera?" Danny chuckled.

Michael looked briefly angry, but it flashed past instantly and he smiled, "No I can make it better. I just need to hold the ring for a few moments."

"What do you mean, better?"

"Well, I don't exactly control the outcome, but I can change things by holding objects. So, if I hold the ring, I can change what's happening so your wife won't be with your friend anymore." Michael reached out his hand, "I'll do it for you, as a thank you for taking me in."

"You're raving mate. I give you my ring and my wife will come back? Yeah right, and I'm a parrot!" Danny snorted.

"No, she may not come back, I don't know that. As I said I can't control the outcome, but I can change it so she won't be with him. What she does from there is unknown. Would you like me to try?"

Danny blew out air in disbelief but handed over his ring.

"Go for it mate, can't hurt can it?"

He shook his head and went back out to the kitchen to check the pizzas. As he slid them back in for a few more moments, it occurred to him that his ring was worth a few hundred pounds and that he may just have fallen for a ridiculous scam. It was unlikely, as Michael could have just run off when he first found it, but Danny went back to check anyway.

The living room was empty. No Michael. His ring was on the table though and a note which said;

'Tow truck arrived earlier than expected. Result! Thanks for everything. I did the thing with the ring. Good luck!'

It took several moments for Danny to take in that all of this had happened in the couple of minutes he was in the kitchen, but in truth he was just relieved that the peculiar man was out of his house.

He slipped his ring back on, more from habit than anything else and the second he did, his phone rang. Even though he knew it was crazy, his heart jumped that it might be Erin and Michael's weird little plan had worked. But the number wasn't Erin's, it was unknown.

"Hello?" he answered.

"Mr Carr, Mr Danny Carr?"

"Yes."

"It's the police Mr Carr. Is your wife's name Erin?"

Danny felt cold pins and needles start in the back of his head.

"Er, yes. She's left me, but yes."

"Oh. When was this?"

"She left yesterday morning, why?"

"And your address is Castle House, Crag Lane, New Granton?"

"Yes. Why? What's going on?"

Danny felt the pause at the other end of the line and his hands started to shake, then eventually, "Well, I'm really sorry to tell you this Mr Carr, but your wife was found dead about an hour ago."

"What? What do you mean?"

"She was driving home by the looks of things. She was at the end of Crag Lane. She must have skidded off the road, and I'm really sorry but it looks like she may have been there since yesterday afternoon."

There was another pause, then the man added gently, "I have to say, it didn't look like she had left you, she was pointing towards your house, there was a meal for two in the passenger seat, and ..." a further pause, "Some new baby clothes. Was she pregnant?"

Danny slid to the floor, the phone falling from his hand as the policemen carried on talking, so he didn't hear the next words, "Also, again sorry to ask, but do you know a Bill James? He was found dead at his home last night after a probable overdose. I only ask because your wife's number was the last on his call list?"

QA Greenbaum

*Q*A Greenbaum, or Quincy Abraham Greenbaum , to give him his full title was the best, the best in the business. If you wanted a certain service with no questions asked and a one hundred per cent guarantee, then he was your man.

Standing six feet four tall, his athletic frame told you he was in control. Blue eyes looked into your very soul and his voice was as smooth and enjoyable as Bourbon with ice.

Removing his jacket, Greenbaum rolled up his sleeves before we discussed business and I pitied the person who had given him the scars on his left forearm. He loved the number seventeen and that's why he always wanted one point seven million per contract. But it was worth that amount just to see my husband dead; and besides, I'd get his full forty five million dollar fortune.

"It's quite a story, the start of a bestselling novel maybe?"

"I suppose so. Yes, I suppose so, if you analyse it from that perspective." Bethany Richards replied to the question posed by Doctor Killigan.

"Relax, there's no catch. Drink?"

"I'll just have a coffee, white, no sugar."

"Bethany, Beth, you're long passed the interview stage. Perhaps something a little stronger, besides it's Christmas Eve."

"Oh no thanks, a coffee will be fine. I have to drive home later."

"You could always take a cab."

"No thanks, Doctor Killigan, I prefer to drive."

"Doctor Killigan?" he laughed, "Please Beth, call me Paul, it's Christmas Eve."

Savouring the aroma for a moment, Bethany Richards tasted her coffee. She'd worked at Thorngate Asylum for just over six months and this was her first Christmas at the infamous building. Thoughts and questions raced through her mind as Doctor Paul Killigan flirted with her.

She'd known from the very beginning about his reputation with the female staff, but that had never put her off. Just like him, Bethany had longed to work at the asylum and had excelled throughout her time at University. And just like Paul Killigan she had landed a job at Thorngate at the age of twenty five; he'd served the place for thirty years.

Snow still fell lightly outside, so Beth didn't refuse a second coffee. Glancing at the clock, the young psychiatrist set a deadline for seven forty- five. The charming, seductive onslaught moved up a gear and she knew his eyes undressed her.

"So what do you make of it?"

Paul Killigan laughed as Bethany Richards waved the papers at him.

"Run of the mill stuff, Beth, run of the mill stuff." Taking the papers as he spoke, he gave them a brief glance.

"QA Greenbaum? Questions and answers, Maud Green. Easy stuff, Beth. We all know Maud loves to change the letter D for a letter B. The rest, all this Quincey stuff, money and Bourbon, it's all pure fiction. Fiction from the star of the show, our very own Maud Green."

The conversation continued, the snow started to fall heavier and Beth's deadline moved forward by fifteen minutes when Paul Killigan's hands started to switch between her shoulders and buttocks.

XXX

Joe waved as Bethany approached and the security gate swung open. Wishing each other a Merry Christmas through the driver's window, she shut out the falling snow with the touch of a button and turned up the radio. The roads were slowly getting worse, but still driveable.

Maud Green, Bethany thought. *She certainly was the star of the show and a damn good reason to work at Thorngate Asylum.*

XXX

Maud Green was born on the third of April, along with her twin sister Isabelle, in nineteen fifty- seven. Their mother was a small, unassuming woman who lived only to serve her husband. He was a tall, athletic, god- preaching man of the church. From an early age she'd shown an interest in the occult and her father had regularly tried to beat it out of her. Isabelle was the opposite, the perfect child, and people often said it was a case of good versus evil. Maud made no friends at school and was a victim of bullying. Her father asked for the help of others in the church when his daughter acquired a Ouija board and began speaking of a bad demon. She often wrote these two words wherever and whenever she could; it was also the start of Maud Green switching the letters D and B. At this point her father, the Reverend Green, decided to take her out of school.

Many teachers came to home school Maud, but quickly left. Strange things began to happen and most of the people willing to undertake the educational task needed professional counselling and soon moved out of the area, Padlocks were placed on the door to her quarters and the rooms were stripped to the bare minimum because of the ever more frequent violent and unexplainable episodes. Maud no longer spoke, she only communicated through writing. Elaborate stories followed, names invented and secret messages were cleverly woven into words. Over the years she had less and less human contact and eventually only five people saw her on a regular basis.

It all ended on the eighteenth of May, nineteen seventy- four. Maud escaped and went on a wild, killing spree. Her mother died first and then three of her friends. Neighbours tried to help, but they too fell to the blood- soaked frenzy.

Her father's church was set alight and as people tried to stop the killings and madness, they too became victims. Reverend Green fell to his knees and asked for forgiveness. But Isabelle entered the church to confront her sister.

Only one sister was found alive in the burnt wreckage, Maud, but her sibling's body was never found. The words *Bad Demon* were written in blood on the surviving walls and Maud was standing naked at the scorched font, laughing insanely.

An extensive search never revealed the whereabouts of Isabelle's body and no knife was ever found. Some witnesses stated that Maud *was* carrying a knife and others stated that she carried out the killings with her bare hands. Others said that a dark figure stood at her side the whole time. The news soon spread around the world and became known as 'The Bad Demon Murders'. The trial lasted six weeks and at the age of seventeen, Maud Green was sent to Thorngate Asylum. Forty- five years later and she's still there, still communicating through her writings and never to be released.

XXX

December 29th

Ray Guineaman – Humer QC Dead. The headline's impact slowly surged through Bethany Richard's body. Each word slowly separated into individual letters and then reformed into another name. It was so easy and clear. It had become second nature since beginning work at the asylum.

Ray Guineaman – Humer QC Dead was an anagram of Quincey Abraham Greenbaum. Beth sat down. She calmed herself for a few moments, then stood, walked over to the window, then sat down again. Minutes passed, rising once more, she made her way to the fridge, took out the half bottle of white, sat down and started to drink. An unusual breakfast and no glass was needed.

More and more information surged through her mind as she continued to read.

The TV was switched on and all the news channels were broadcasting live from the crime scene.

Guineaman – Humer was known throughout the world. He became the youngest ever QC in England. Retired, moved to the USA in the early sixties and carved out a name and reputation for himself when he set up his own legal firm.

Ray Guineaman – Humer represented some of the biggest names in films, TV, music and business. He was also involved in the Maud Green, `Bad Demon Murders` and he *never* lost.

The world, along with Bethany Richards, was now taking in the fact that he was dead and *Bad Demon* was sprawled all over the walls of his mansion. Evidence had supposedly been found indicating that he was linked to an underage sex racket with links to the church. But most people wanted to know if Maud Green was innocent , and if so, who was `The Bad Demon Killer`?

XXX

The following year, Christmas Day

Bethany Richards drove into the grounds of Thorngate Asylum along with another woman. The case, watched by the world, had finally been brought to a conclusion. After new evidence, new witnesses and various retrials, it was finally over.

Ray Guineaman – Humer was found guilty of underage sex, withholding evidence, bribery and a whole host of other things that wiped out his glittering, God- like career. He`d also raped Maud Green, making her pregnant (Maud`s father had died twenty years ago, but did play a part in the sex racket). New DNA evidence had proven that the scars on Humer`s left forearm had been caused by Maud`s biting and scratching.

Maud was only seventeen when she had given birth. The baby was a healthy girl who had survived, given birth herself and named the child Bethany Richards. She was also the sole benefactor of a forty- five million dollar fortune.

The debate continued with regards to whether Maud Green was innocent and if so, who was the real killer. That legal argument would continue for a while and it was highly unlikely that she`d ever be released.

Beth reached the end of the corridor and her pass opened the two security doors. Only one more door remained. Behind it lived Maud Green, a woman who hadn`t spoken in over fifty years; a woman who still raised questions like, is she good or is she pure evil? Beth Richard`s pass opened the final door and the woman still making newspaper headlines sat looking out of the window.

"Finally, my girls are here." Maud Green spoke and Bethany, along with her mother, just held hands and listened.

"It's starting to snow, I like snow. But I bet you like your bank account better," she laughed out loud.

"Come and sit with me, and watch the snow. We are finally complete, finally three and therefore strong. A coven is always stronger when it's three. Finally, finally we can bring that bad demon under control. Merry Christmas girls, Merry Christmas."

The Robin's Christmas Adventure

Silver mist hovered over the world that particular day. Trees shone pure white and cobwebs gleamed with tiny water drops hanging off the edge. The whole world was silent, apart from a crystal river shimmering and sparkling like a star. Even birds didn't wake from their nests that morning to sing their sweet songs, as the atmosphere was too cold for even their cosy feathers. The frost rested on rooftops and watched over the foggy town. Nobody wanted to go outside that day.

But this lifeless atmosphere did not stop one creature. A tiny robin emerged from its long rest and flew out into the sky. His angelic wings acted like a fluffy coat, held his little body and helped him travel gracefully in the air.

Within what felt like a second, it began to snow slowly. The snowflakes danced beautifully and a huge one broke as it hit the tip of the robin's beak. They reflected and shone like dragon's scales. Although the air started getting colder, the robin didn't give up and still flew above and beyond the tall fir trees.

The robin felt that winter kept following him, as everywhere he flew the trees were frostier. As the tiny bird glided across the sky, he could make out a few people in the main town opening shops and walking around.

He gradually landed on a small post in front of a petite cottage. He sank into the snow and rested, as he was exhausted. The place seemed serene and tranquil and he watched all the glistening snowflakes tumbling down. Unfortunately the quiet, relaxed atmosphere didn't last too long. He heard muffled voices in the house, before the door opened and a young couple walked out shouting at each other.

"I don't understand why you had to keep it a secret!" The lady said.

"It was meant to be a surprise!" The man told her.

"You are the worst husband in the world!" The lady argued.

"Why do you keep doing this?" The man asked her, his voice becoming rather rough.

"So it's my fault, is it? Michael, this was meant to be the perfect Christmas and you always spoil it!"

The tiny robin couldn't take it any longer and he flew away hurriedly. At this time of year, it was always joyful and magical. Songs would be sung, lights would be lit and decorations would be hung all over the place to celebrate Christmas. But it was also a time of stress, where people hurried to buy certain gifts, rushed to cook selected foods and would argue and cry over the chaos of it all. The robin hated that side of Christmas, as he disliked it when people were upset. It made him feel upset too.

As he flew into the main town, he saw huge Christmas fairy lights strung all over the trees, buildings and in shop windows. Warm golds, cooling silvers, hot reds and calm greens created a happy Christmas atmosphere. Hints of both light and dark blues were used for a more chilling effect.

The robin had a huge love for these lights. He looked down on the humongous landscape and noticed more people emerging from their houses and onto the streets with fur coats, woolly gloves, hats and elongated scarves wrapped around their necks.

Lots of children were already getting creative and started making snowmen and having snowball fights. The robin decided to plummet to the ground and watch the fun, to take his mind off the incident he witnessed a few minutes beforehand.

As he landed, he noticed a homeless man sat on the streets. This man had no woolly hat or scarf to keep him warm. He did have a coat, but it was very thin and he was shivering. His tiny cup, to receive money, was empty. Many people walked past without a care. If only the little robin could speak in a language humans could understand, then he could make them rethink their choices, but all he could do was sit and watch.

The homeless man noticed the robin and gave him a sad smile.

"I have nothing on me," the men began, "I wish I did."

The robin moved his head slightly and started to sing a soft song. Even though he didn't have anything to give to the poor man, he thought maybe a tune would make the man happy, even if he smiled for only a second.

And that's what he did; slowly, the man's mouth transformed into a smile.

"You're a clever little birdie. You seem to know music better than I do."

As the man started humming along, the robin knew he should be heading off. He flew into the open air, his wings spread out like a hawk. On either side of him, the decorations shone and he could see shop owners hanging tinsel on the windows. Although he loved this Christmas spirit, he couldn't help feeling heartbroken at what he also witnessed. To think that there's people that don't experience the same joy of Christmas just hurt the little robin's feelings.

He ended his travels by a large house. The reason why he stopped outside this one was because it was different to any other on the street. Whilst the other houses were filled with joy and Christmas spirit, this house looked alone, gloomy and lacking any kind of joy. The only sense of life this house had was the smoke tumbling out of the chimney, like dragon's breath.

The robin decided to be nosey and have a sneaky peak in the window. When he did, he noticed an old man holding a walking cane, in his front room looking at photos of family. The man did not look happy at all, he looked rather upset.

"I guess they won't visit me this year. They didn't come last year either."

This old man needed somebody. The robin wondered why his family weren't going to see him, or wouldn't see him. Nobody should feel isolated at all, should they?

The robin thought of how he could help the old gentleman, but what could a bird do? Instead, he decided to whistle another song, hoping the man would hear him.

The window was slightly ajar, so he didn't need to sing that loud to get the man's attention. The man gave him a big smile and walked up to the window, he gave a small chuckle and opened the window further, so he could lean out and talk to the robin.

"Hello there," the man gave a wave. "You are one cute birdie, aren't you? I must have forgotten to close my window. Oh! Wait there."

The man walked to his small living room table and grabbed the old fashioned tin that was placed on it. As he speed walked to the window, he opened it up and took out a small homemade biscuit. He broke a bit off and placed a large crumb on the tiny wall next to the window, for the robin.

"I bet you'll have a lovely Christmas filled with joy and your family."

The robin listened as he took a few beak-fulls of the biscuit.

"You're enjoying it? I made them myself since I can't make anything else. I'd give anything for a slice of Christmas cake. Oh!! That's the phone!! Goodbye little birdie."

The man left the room and the robin stayed to finish his snack. Even though the man was lonely, he was kind enough to give him a little bit of a biscuit. The robin felt flattered, but wished he could do more than sing for these people.

They only see what's on the outside, a sweet bird, but he can't speak to humans or do anything for them, so they don't see anything else. But the robin knew he just had to deal with it. He finished his little snack and flew away into the sky.

What a day it had been. Every minute kept getting worse. He saw more of the homeless almost dying from the cold, he heard more arguments and he saw even lonelier, stressed- out people. No one seemed to be happy that day. This really did bring his Christmas spirit down as fast as a blustering tornado.

But what was this? He heard a loud ringing sound coming from the church. The sound of those bells echoed through the town as loud as thunder

He glided across the sky like an ice skater and soared around the buildings and trees. The smiling sun shone brightly and huge rays glistened across the sky. He landed on a small log and waited, as the bells still rang.

All of a sudden, the doors burst open and out came a bride and groom. The bride's white dress flew behind her, and ruffles that looked like white snowflakes draped down her lacy dress.

The bird's heart smiled and he clapped his wings together in applause. This was the start of the Christmas he knew, the time of love and happiness commencing. Without even thinking about it, his wings flapped upwards and onward excitedly, and he moved towards the bride and groom. He gave a little tweet and the couple smiled back.

"Hello, little birdie," the bride said to him.

"Aw isn't he sweet?!" She said to the groom.

The robin was overjoyed as he sang again, before he left them both. They gave him a small wave and he caught a nice whiff of the eucalyptus leaves she used in her bouquet of flowers.

As he flew off again, he passed the house where the old man lived and when he quickly glanced through the window, he saw the old man was feeling his best. The people who were in his photographs were there in front of him, handing him a lovely Christmas cake with marzipan and Wensleydale cheese.

Finally, the Christmas spirit had begun floating about and creating magic. More houses were decorated with Christmas trees and baubles. As he went back into the main town, the homeless people he had seen before were tucking into sandwiches and sipping cups of freshly made tea. Was this a miracle? Christmas was really happening and the robin felt delighted.

A large number of people had joined up and made a choir. They were singing Christmas songs and making shoppers feel really upbeat. The robin flew down next to them and listened carefully. The music made him feel so much joy and he even bobbed his head in time with the music. He enjoyed listening to them every year.

As the choir carried on singing, the robin noticed that the homeless man he had seen earlier that morning was talking to three people; a young couple and their small daughter.

The robin decided to investigate this and flew to them. He hid behind a dustbin

and watched them. He was shocked. The young couple were the two people he first saw arguing that morning. They seemed to have calmed down
and were delighted to be in each other's company. The homeless man was holding a sandwich and a piping hot cup of tea.

"I can't thank you enough for this," the man said to them, "I'm so thankful."

"We've been giving sandwiches and drinks to all the homeless people," the young lady responded. "We like to give during Christmas."

"Exactly, no one should be alone during Christmas," the man said as he put his arm around his wife.

"Bless you all," the homeless man said. "Thank you very much."

The robin decided to make an appearance and he jumped towards them as if he was a ballerina.

"Hello again," the homeless man waved to him.

The robin replied to him with music. All four of them smiled and listened. The bird knew that it would be getting dark soon, so it would be his bedtime. He was starting to feel the chills of the snowy weather and decided that even though the atmosphere was wonderful and he could stay there and dance forever, a warm and cosy nest would be a lovely place to be.

So off he flew, leaving the carol singers singing, the couple giving and the shoppers shopping. He flew back through the snowflakes. His journey was harder as the wind was trying to push and entice him to enjoy the Christmas music.

But the robin fought through the difficult weather and managed to get back to his home. What was once a river that morning had transformed completely into ice. The ground had turned into a blanket of snow, the cobwebs had a mesmerising shine on the trees and he could just about see the mountains in the distance that he could not see in the misty morning. Any water drops that were alive before had changed into icicles and were glistening in the remaining light.

The robin found his home, a tree with only a few of the autumnal conkers on. He buried himself into the single hole in the bark of the tree, and scurried inside the nest he made all by himself out of twigs and leaves, so he could hide inside
and embedded himself away from the harsh winter weather. As he got comfy, he wondered what adventures he'd be up to the next day.

A Winter's Tale

Mrs Christmas lived with her husband Nicolas in a beautiful cottage in the village of Drummond in Scotland. Mr Christmas had a butcher's shop called 'Meat and Greet'. He loved his work and was a popular figure amongst all the villagers.

Mrs Christmas adored children, but sadly never had any of her own. She helped her husband in the shop a few days a week and organised many events in the village hall. She loved knitting and would donate everything she made to the local charity shop.

After twenty five years of marriage they were still very happy and were looking forward to spending the rest of their lives together. And then Mr Christmas suffered a terrible accident with the bacon slicer. By the time his wife found him it was too late, he was dead.

Mrs Christmas was very sad and locked herself away for the next two years. She employed a local man to run the shop and rarely ventured out of the cottage. Gradually Mrs Christmas started to get involved in the community again and promised to do some baking for the Christmas fair.

The week before Christmas a heavy snow shower had covered the roads around the cottage, so Mrs Christmas decided she would stay at home and get on with some knitting.

It was already dark at 4 o'-clock. Mrs Christmas was sitting in her old green armchair winding her wool into neat balls. The fire was crackling in the corner and lovely carols were playing on the radio. She walked over to the window intending to draw the curtains, but before she could do so she noticed a small child shivering in the snow. She quickly opened the door and beckoned her inside.

"Oh come in, come in my dear. I'm just making some mince pies."

She grasped the child's hand and led her into the room.

"What's your name?" She asked, smiling warmly.

Sharon's face lit up as she whispered shyly.

"My name's Sharon. Are you really Mrs Christmas?"

"Of course my dear":

She reassured the little girl.

"Come and get cosy by the fire whilst I put the oven on. Would you like some lemonade?"

"Oh yes please Mrs Christmas" she replied grinning.

She had decided to make lots of mince pies to sell at the fair this year. It was about time that she made some money for herself.

Since her husband's death nobody had really helped her, but now she had the chance to make a bit of extra money to make her own life more comfortable.

The next morning she woke from a deep sleep, still exhausted from all the cleaning up she'd done yesterday. She smiled as she saw how spotless the cottage looked. But there was no sign of Sharon, just several boxes of mince pies neatly packed ready to be taken to the fair.

She relit the fire and ate her breakfast feeling really pleased with herself. She was sure she'd make a tidy sum later from her delicious pies. As she was stacking the boxes into the car, a woman approached her. She had tears streaming down her face and was clutching something in her hand. As she came closer Mrs Christmas became concerned.

"Oh, hello Mrs Christmas" she sobbed, "My Sharon is missing. Her bed hasn't been slept in. She's never run away for this long before. Have you seen her?"

Mrs Green showed her a photo of Sharon.

"Oh! You poor soul," Mrs Christmas's eyes softened.

"Oh, come here my dear."

She hugged her tightly, smiling to herself.

"I'm afraid not, but I'll keep an eye out for her. I'm just on my way to take some pies to the village hall. Can I drop you off in the village?"

Mrs Green nodded and got in the passenger seat.

"Don't worry my dear, I'm sure she'll turn up soon."

Mrs Christmas parked outside the village hall and watched as Mrs Green made her way home. She unloaded the boxes and left them in the hall kitchen, her nose wrinkled with pleasure at the sweet aroma still lingering in the car.

Later that week there was a faint knock on the door.

"Who is it?" Mrs Christmas shouted.

A little voice replied. "Hello, are you Mrs Christmas?"

As she opened the door, a beautiful little girl with long blond hair and blue eyes smiled back at her.

"Oh my dear, come in you are so welcome. Come and sit near the fire and get warm. I'll make you a hot chocolate, would you like that?"

"Yes please Mrs Christmas."

"What's your name dear?"

"Tracey," she replied.

Mrs Christmas sat in her armchair and stroked Tracey's hair, her eyes misting over.

"That's a lovely name my dear."

She remembered her own mother sat in this same chair, brushing her long blonde hair and singing to her; all those wonderful memories of childhood when she felt true happiness. If only she could be that child again, safe in her mother's arms.

"Why are you sad Mrs Christmas? Tracey asked.

"Oh, I was just thinking about my mother, my dear. She used to sing to me whilst she brushed my hair, just where you are sitting right now."

"Where is she now then?"

"Oh, she just left one day. My father searched everywhere for her, but she never returned. Drink up there's more hot chocolate on the stove and the mince pies should be nice and warm by now."

Storm

*R*ain poured mercilessly. Torrents of water flooded. Gullies struggled to swallow. Lightning danced across the black sky, accompanied by an orchestra of thunder. The once mighty oak, which marked the centre of the woodland, stood shattered, smouldering, wounded from the destructive lightning bolt which had destroyed its three hundred year life.

Only one watched; naked, flesh ignorant of the cold, wet night.
Not many who now walked the earth would know her name, but there was one and she could sense his presence. Once lovers, but now the taste of revenge was sweet upon her lips.

She moved cat- like across the mulch and wet fallen branches, stopping at a clearing to listen to a `last orders drunk` that had dropped his mobile phone. As eyes met, his words never escaped. Blood spilled from the drunk`s mouth and eyes and he too fell to the floor just like the branches. Gripping the red rose in her left hand, blood trickled down the fingers of her soft white hand, matching the colour of the petals. Thorns pierced deeper and the river of red seductively ran over curvaceous thighs and pooled at the feet of the goddess.

XXX

Yorkshire was a long drive from London, especially in the storm which had descended on the UK. Tyres tore up the miles on the motorway. The coffee and cheeseburgers all tasted equally crap at each individual service station, and were all equally over expensive.

No sane person would believe a single word of his story, but he knew it to be true. All the research, the dates, the signs, they all led to one conclusion and to one place.

XXX

The storm had eased, but rain still fell lightly. Three men emerged from an old abandoned garage, which stood by the iron bridge. Fuelled by drugs and alcohol, they needed little encouragement when they saw the female approaching. Her naked form excited them. Rain trickled over pale flesh, soaked, raven black hair clung to her back and shoulders, wild green eyes invited them all and as she teasingly fondled her breasts, she let out uncontrollable laughter. She was Nalini, Goddess of the Holly Bush and to walk the earth once more felt good.

Alcohol and drugs coursed through her veins, she relished in the taste of a kiss and gave no resistance when human hands traced and touched her body. They all laughed, drank more cheap drink and let the effects of needle infused pleasure ride through their veins like an endless climax. Their names were insignificant, only hers mattered. Soon, all were naked, chanting, lost in a frenzy of wild, ancient traditions. "Nalini, Nalini, Nalini," all three males worshipped. "Nalini, Nalini, Nalini." The chanting continued.

XXX

Four more miles the Sat Nav said. Professor Aidan Webster had spent all his life waiting for this moment. Excitement surged through hm. He'd studied all religions, beliefs, cultures and civilisations. Professor Webster couldn't help laughing, he laughed and banged the steering wheel. Decades of study had led him to travel to distant lands Ancient books and scrolls had been translated and he'd waited patiently. Symbols and paintings from caves had all been studied and brought to conclusion. The Professor hummed a little tune, pulled over, parked the car and grabbed his coat.

XXX

As the naked bodies danced, chanted and indulged, night rain continued to fall. Manic laughter heralded the debauchery to a climax. Screams accompanied the laughter as the men writhed in agony. Jerking in spasms, they clung to their eyes and mouths as blood poured once more. The ancient goddess bathed in their slow, painful deaths, splashing her hair and body with the red liquid of life.

As Nalini rose to her feet, she offered up her arms and green lightning danced to her command above. Clutching the red rose once more, she closed her eyes and recited an ancient prayer.

Professor Webster looked on. Words escaped him. His life's work had come to this. Emotions flooded him and he just continued to watch. Nalini's eyes opened and she immediately met the stare of her new admirer. Smiling, she offered no malice, a hand beckoned him and he instantly responded. Lips met and they both enjoyed a sensuous kiss.

"I knew you would come." The Goddess spoke.
Webster offered no reply.
"It was always your destiny."
The two continued to kiss and then a new voice spoke.
"Nalini, you look as beautiful as ever."
"Delgu," pushing away the Professor, Nalini replied.
Anger rose within her, but not for long. His deep blue eyes looked at her longingly; his red mane was tied back with the broach she had made for him over a

thousand years ago and ancient, purple symbols adorned his upper torso.

"And why do I have the pleasure of the God of snow and ice?" For the first time her voice was soft and calm.

"I will always love you Nalini."

"And I can never forgive you Delgu."

"Thousands of years have passed."

"And they will continue to do so."

"You still have the rose."

"Forever."

"Then you will remember me."

"Always."

For a moment the two were lost in thoughts of better times.

"He is yours." Nalini pointed to Aidan Webster. She took the ancient book from inside his jacket pocket. The Goddess wrapped the ancient writings in leaf and bark to honour traditions and smiled at the thought of someone finding it.

Professor Webster backed away slightly, but Delgu's powerful hand soon rested on his shoulder. As the two locked eyes, Aidan Webster needed no explanation. He knew they were two immortals, existing long before Celtic times, long before all known religions and beliefs. He'd had the ancient scrolls translated, he knew that they were once lovers and that he'd betrayed her by sleeping with another. In her anger she swore an oath to walk the earth, taking the blood of humans. Delgu has always needed the sacrifice of humans in order to bring the snow and ice. He needed the bones of the mortals, the stronger the belief in the Gods and Goddesses the harsher the winter. But Webster also knew that love had prevailed in the end. Nalini knew Delgu's secret and had the power to destroy him. This she had vowed to do the next time they met. But she still carried the blood rose he had given to her on their first date and as today had proved, when they did finally meet once more, she couldn't bring herself to speak the ancient words that would kill a God.

Pain surged through the Professor's shoulder, spreading throughout his body. As flesh peeled away, blood curdling screams were enjoyed by the once lovers. Bones turned to dust and on Delgu's command ascended to the clouds. Nalini's eyes glowed a bright green and fire consumed the pulpy, human mass of flesh and blood, leaving no remains.

For a moment the two immortals nearly kissed. But Nalini smiled, picked up her rose and walked away. Lightning danced across the sky once more and then she was gone. Delgu closed his eyes. A swirling ball of snow and ice consumed him, which in turn joined the clouds above.

XXX

In the morning, villagers gathered to take pictures of the shattered oak tree. This story was told for decades and beyond, along with the tale of the lightning storm. The police launched a search for the missing people of the village and after a while they became just another unsolved case. When Professor Aidan Webster's family realized he was missing, they alerted the authorities and he too became another unsolved case. But his sister moved to Yorkshire and relentlessly continued the search until she sadly died of a rare disease.

But the winter of that year was a particularly good one for the Yorkshire village. All the holly bushes bore beautiful red berries in abundance and the villagers frequently passed comment on what a wonderful shade of red they were. The snow never seemed to stop falling and the village pond froze over. All the village children, and some of the more adventurous adults, enjoyed sledging and skating for weeks. And that story was passed down from generation to generation so that it would never be forgotten.

Jamie And The Gingerbread Man

*O*utside the winter weather really had arrived. The crisp, white snow blanketed the earth for miles around. Inside, the fire crackled in the hearth. The air was filled with the warm fragrance of freshly baked cinnamon bread. Young Jamie was wearing his favourite pyjamas and clutching a battered old teddy. His mother smiled as she remembered that same teddy bear when she unwrapped her Christmas present all those many years before.

Jamie and his mother now lived on their own after his father had died twelve months ago. The only other remaining member of the family was Jamie's grandmother who lived many miles away.

Although Jamie was an only child, his mother had always made sure that she allowed him the freedom that she'd enjoyed as a child. They didn't have any close neighbours and they were quite isolated, but he was a sensible boy and understood about the dangers of wandering too far from home. He was excited by the sight of all that snow and the thought of being able to play in it.

After breakfast Jamie dressed in his warmest clothes, happy at the prospect of playing outdoors. He pulled on his wellington boots over his thick red socks, donned his winter coat and finally his brand-new hat, scarf and gloves that his grandmother had sent him for Christmas. Jamie's mother bent down to give him a hug and as she did, she slipped a gingerbread man into the deep pocket of his duffle coat.

"Don't wander too far from the house," were the last words she spoke.

"I won't," he said as he stepped out onto the crunchy snow.

Jamie laughed as a flake of snow landed on his nose. He stuck out his tongue and let another snowflake melt on it. Today was going to be amazing, he thought to himself.

Firstly, Jamie set about making a snowman. He was surprised to see how quickly a small snowball became a huge boulder for the snowman's body. The head took half as long and was soon put in place. Two lumps of coal made striking eyes, a pine cone made a great knobbly nose and some conkers provided perfect brown teeth! To finish off, he took off his scarf and wrapped it around the snowman's neck. Jamie stood back and was pleased with his handiwork.

Next, Jamie lay down on a snow-covered bank and moved his arms and legs to create a snow angel just like his mother had shown him. Once again, he was pleased with the result.

Jamie decided that it was time to explore and see more of this magical winter wonderland whilst he could. No doubt the snow would soon melt, and he had to make the most of it. He hopped and jumped into deep snow drifts leaving a series of large holes. Then he took huge strides across the ground leaving clear footprints behind him.

Time quickly passed by and Jamie was enjoying every minute of his adventure. He felt like an explorer discovering a whole new world. He didn't realise how long he'd been walking. He had often gone this far before, but the strangeness of the land made it less familiar. It seemed unusually scary. The air was damp, the silence close and deep. He turned around to retrace his steps, but the snow had shifted and covered his tracks. He looked about for any recognizable landmark, but there was nothing. The sky was getting darker and Jamie felt afraid. If only he'd brought along the compass that had belonged to his father.

Jamie was a born survivor. Pulling his hat firmly down over his ears, he set off walking in the hope that he would soon spot something familiar.

Very shortly he came across a fallen log. His heart sank. He hadn't passed this way earlier. He sat down and sighed then sank his now cold hands into his coat pocket.

He was surprised when he discovered something there. He smiled when he pulled out the gingerbread man. Then he began to cry when he thought about the day before when he and his mummy were in their nice warm kitchen. He remembered gently placing currants on gingerbread faces and laughing at the one that looked slightly cross-eyed and down in the mouth. This was the one he was now holding.

He remembered the words of the rhyme his mother had taught him:

"Run, run, run as fast as you can. You'll never catch me, I'm the gingerbread man."

Tears fell faster and faster, dropping one by one onto the gingerbread man. To Jamie's surprise the gingerbread man appeared to wink an eye and smile. Jamie jumped to his feet and the gingerbread man fell to the ground. Jamie's eyes widened as the gingerbread man started to grow and grow until they were both the same height. His currant eyes were now like lumps of coal and his mouth had definitely turned upwards.

The gingerbread man took hold of Jamie's hand before lifting him gently onto his shoulders. With long strides they were soon moving quickly across the snowy countryside. Jamie felt safe and fell fast asleep. Jamie awoke to find himself back home and on the armchair next to the fire. He was wearing his pyjamas, clutching his teddy and was covered with a warm red blanket. Beside him, on the coffee table, was a glass of milk and a plate with a gingerbread man on it. Jamie was sure that one of the currant eyes winked at him.

Jamie wondered if it had all been a dream, or had it really been magic?

Mistletoe and Whine

*L*ike a conductor, she waved her hands and her orchestra of employees got to work, turning their little shop into a winter wonderland. Well, there were only two others with her, but nonetheless the job got done. Tinsel wrapped around the till and baubles hung from the shelves.

This was the one joy of Christmas in retail, before the hustle and bustle of consumers filed through the doors and down the aisles. But still, there was no reason to complain; it filled the till with money and made customers smile.

Feeling a vibration in her pocket, Annabelle, the shop manager, stole a quick glance at her phone. Her heart sank. It was Josh, for the third time that weekend. The call went to voicemail; once a lover, now a stranger.

Losing love was easy, like letting go of a balloon. It flew away with little chance of coming back, especially around Christmas time when the world was taken over by frenzy and panic; people were blinded and forgot what was truly important. It was cold outside, with snow falling from the heavens. It was warmer inside people's homes, with the gentle roar of log fires; but freezing in one's heart, where betrayal and anger intermingled easily.

But it was something Annabelle couldn't help. It wasn't her fault love never worked in her favour. She was restless, like a toddler at 4am ready for adventure, when the rest of the world still slept. She loved experimenting, it ran in her family.

However, this only endangered the men she promised to take under her wing. Annabelle broke hearts, not always deliberately, but it was a curse she had inherited. Changing from one man to another was easy.

Just like Lisa was changing the snow globes and nutcrackers round on the shelf. It made Annabelle shudder; there were some things she didn't want changing.

Holding back a tone of annoyance, she asked Isaac to give Lisa a hand, and he was more than happy to put his tinsel shenanigans on hold to help. It was crystal clear that Isaac would do anything for Annabelle and she liked to think she knew why. Despite Annabelle having no interest in dating an employee, she didn't shut Isaac down; she was just keeping her options open.

The large clock on the wall grabbed Annabelle's attention; 10:55am. The shop was closed to the public whilst the Christmas decor was being assembled. It was beautiful, but reminded Annabelle of the upcoming tiring `seven days a week` management, when her shop would open on Sundays throughout December.

"Shall we call it a day?" Annabelle asked, clearing her throat. "I know we're supposed to be here until one, but we all have places to be."

Lisa beamed. "You're the best!"

Compliments were Annabelle's favourite thing to receive and she couldn't stop her lips twitching into a smile. It was a small gesture, but Annabelle liked to know what her employees were up to; for rota and conversational purposes. For example, that afternoon Lisa was finishing some shopping and Isaac was taking his brothers bowling.

"What are you doing today, Annie?" Lisa asked.

"Or, who?"

Annabelle pretended to swat Lisa, before sighing.

"I'm meeting my stepmother."

"Oohh!" Isaac waved his hands like he was imitating a ghost.

"The Witch!"

Laughter echoed around the room. As boss, Annabelle understood the boundaries of what she should or shouldn't say to her employees. After all, they weren't her friends. Still, it was comforting to confide in them when she struggled with her stepmother's antics, who'd unknowingly earned herself the nickname, `The Witch`, when waltzing into the shop one day wearing only green.

"Does anyone fancy going for a drink tonight?" Lisa asked, wrapping tinsel around her arm absentmindedly.

Isaac furrowed his eyebrows. "A crowded bar with too small a drinks at too high a price?"

"I thought we could just go to the pub at the end of the street?"

Isaac's face softened, "Oh, sure! I'll be free after seven."

Lisa turned to Annabelle, "You coming, Annie?"

"I'll think about it,"

Annabelle responded, forcing a smile through tightened lips, knowing she had every intention of not going. Time with her stepmother was draining physically and emotionally; it took Annabelle at least two days to recover.

After Lisa and Isaac left, Annabelle grabbed her handbag, stopping under the mistletoe at the door to take one last look. Her arts and craft shop, her pride and joy, had been transformed. Not overwhelmingly breath-taking like she had envisioned, but still spectacular.

The only difference compared to last year was the lack of cotton snow, as it made Lisa sneeze. Annabelle adored the paper snowflakes hanging from the ceiling, which some children at the primary school had created during her recent visit. The snowflakes were decorated with sequins and glitter which reflected in the shop lights, creating dancing kaleidoscopic patterns on the walls.

Outside, real snow was falling. It disappeared upon touching the ground, but filled the air with a sense of magic. The coldness made attempts to crawl up Annabelle's sleeves, so she buried her hands deep in her coat pockets. The more steps she took, the more agitated she became. She was dreading this meeting.

The cafe was quiet and cosy with a few customers, but not so many that it was uncomfortable. Through the tinted window Annabelle caught sight of her stepmother, Louise, a glamorous woman only fifteen years older than Annabelle, which caused discomfort when Annabelle thought about it too deeply. When opening the door, Louise gave Annabelle a big smile and beckoned her over. Annabelle sat down and saw Louise had already bought her a coffee, still steaming.

"Hi Louise," Annabelle began.

"Annabelle-"

"How are you?"

"Do you have a boyfriend yet?"

There it was. Annabelle scowled. "Well, can you believe that? We've already failed the Bechdel test."

It was easy to make light of the subject, but difficult to have this conversation with a woman she'd only known for five years. This was a conversation Annabelle wanted with her real mother. Unfortunately, Annabelle didn't know who that was.

"What about Jacob?" Louise asked, taking hold of her teacup.

Annabelle suddenly recalled the gent she had flirted with at the summer gala. There had been no attraction, but they exchanged numbers. Their texts hadn't made it past square one. She couldn't even remember his face.

"Not my type."

"Carlos?"

"The young Italian who worked two days a week at the shop before returning home, he was ten years younger than me. Louise!"

"How about Antonio?"

"Carlo's dad!" Annabelle couldn't hold back her eye roll.

"He was ten years older than me! I don't take advantage of older men with heartache!"

Louise raised an eyebrow. "Why did you look at me when you said that?"

"I didn't," Annabelle snapped, taking a sip of coffee.

Louise sounded hesitant when she spoke next, as if testing the waters of Annabelle's annoyance.

"Josh?"

Hearing his name made Annabelle's heart drop and her whole being felt heavy. Finding her voice was a struggle.

"He cheated on me."

"Mistakes happen."

"With his ex-wife," Annabelle retorted back.

Annabelle didn't miss Josh; it was the cheating which caused the heartache. It was a touchy subject for Annabelle. Granted she flirted with men and had many phone numbers saved, but she always assured them she wasn't looking for a relationship and checked that they were single before locking their numbers into her phone.

So when Josh asked her to be his girlfriend, she strangely agreed, only to spot him days later getting close to the woman who originally ruined his life.

When Annabelle grew silent, Louise offered a sympathetic smile.

"There must be someone you could spend a romantic Christmas with; you're nearly thirty!"

Annabelle was horrified. "I'm twenty-six!"

"Do you hold back because of your mother?"

Louise knew this was difficult on the whole family; it had taken Annabelle's father months to open up about his first lover. It pained Annabelle to be involved in this unfortunate situation.

Her mother had been wild and free spirited when she met Annabelle's father and the young couple had fallen in love; or Annabelle's father had anyway.

Annabelle's mother didn't commit to anything; bulldozing into people's lives, overstaying her welcome, and then moving on when satisfied. If she accidentally wound up pregnant, she promptly disappeared, leaving the baby with the father; a perfectly planned clockwork routine.

With the possibility she changed her name with every new man she wrapped around her finger, and no photos or birthday cards, Annabelle had no connection to this woman who was meant to be her mother.

"She doesn't matter, she never has," Annabelle scowled, her tone ice cold.

The awkward silence that followed was almost deafening and the two women couldn't make eye contact. Louise drew circles on the table with her acrylic nails whilst her stepdaughter stared blankly into her cold coffee.

"Wine?" Louise finally piped up.

When Annabelle didn't respond, Louise headed to the counter and purchased a bottle of white wine, knowing that was Annabelle's favourite. It was curious that the family-friendly cafe sold wine at Christmas time, but Annabelle understood. After all, she was opening her shop on Sundays again; it was time to take advantage of the festive season and fill the tills however possible.

Over the wine, Louise made conversation about Christmas day, going over the family plans. Annabelle still felt disheartened and occasionally zoned out. Her energy had disintegrated along with her confidence and she felt an emptiness that wine couldn't fill.

"Remember you're bringing the trifle, I'm handling the turkey and your brother and his fiancé are bringing the veg. Your grandma's got the Christmas pudding and she mentioned something about chipolatas too."

It felt like an eternity before Louise announced she was going home. On the way, Louise bought another bottle of wine and handed it to Annabelle, making her promise to contact her if she ever needed anything. Annabelle nodded, but had no intention of going to her stepmother. It was easier to keep everything to herself, that's how she'd always managed.

The women walked in opposite directions, Annabelle at a slower pace than normal despite wanting to get home. She was fed up, had no holiday romance, and felt cold and unwanted during the season where love and joy were meant to be prominent.

"Annie!"

Annabelle heard the familiar voice and looked up to see Lisa heading towards her. People had to step to the side as Lisa passed them with full shopping bags.

"Off to see The Witch?"

Annabelle grinned, feeling sudden warmth.

"I've just been. I survived, but she still wants me to find a date for Christmas." Lisa rolled her eyes.

"Men, they're not worth the hassle! Do you need a drink?"

Annabelle remembered the wine tucked under her arm.

"Shall we go to the shop and share this first? We'll save money at the pub that way."

"Good idea! We can have a good whine before we meet up with Isaac, only if you're sure though?"

Annabelle paused to think. She had just made plans. Did she need a Doctor? But it felt nice, Annabelle knew deep down she didn't want to spend the rest of the day alone, but she couldn't face texting one of the many men she trailed along.

She wanted to spend this time with her friend….colleague…friend?

"I'm sure," Annabelle's smile was genuine, which caused Lisa to clap her hands together and almost drop her bags. Annabelle couldn't help laughing, offering to carry a bag.

Lisa was delighted.

"Hurray! We should make plans more often! Do you have my number?"

Annabelle nodded. "Remember that week in October when you kept showing up late?"

Lisa gulped. "I'm so glad you didn't fire me!"

On the way to the shop, Lisa chatted away, giving Annabelle time to think. Annabelle's life revolved around the shop and her boy troubles and Lisa was like a breath of fresh air. Annabelle made the decision to go through her contacts and have a clear out, although it was a shame she'd have to keep Louise's number; but as long as she had Lisa's.

Lisa would often invite. Annabelle to places; maybe it was time to accept some of those offers, let loose and make some proper friends.

And in regards to the boys Annabelle strung along? Well, that part of the future was still hazy; could she stay away from that bad habit forever? Well, that was what New Year Resolutions were for. Annabelle could always try again next year.

The Doll

*E*very day on her way to school, Sarah had admired the doll at the back of the window. The shop was an old antique shop. In truth, it was more of a second hand `tat` shop than a proper antique shop. The window was jammed packed with all sorts. Strange stuffed animals dominated, their piercing eyes seemed to stare at her and follow her gaze as she pressed her nose to the glass to get a better view of the doll.

"Come on Sarah, we'll be late again, " her mother repeated every time.

She was like a stuck record, her mum. It was a daily ritual, but no matter how much Sarah pleaded with her to buy the doll, her mum was having none of it.

"When you learn to behave yourself and do as you're told, Sarah, maybe I'll think about it"

So that was that then - or was it? Sarah had a plan. In two weeks it would be the start of the long summer holidays. She would earn enough money to pay for the doll herself. But how could she do that?

She was only eight years old, so too young to work in a shop or do a paper round. She always helped her dad clean the car every weekend and they had all the equipment in the garage; sponges, buckets, cloths and car polish. So why not clean cars and make some money? That weekend Sarah pitched her idea to her dad and he agreed it was a great idea.

"As long as you just do the cars on our close that will be fine," he said.

Sarah made up some 'business cards' and posted them through all the letter boxes on the street. There were over fifty in total, so as long as she got at least ten responses at five pound each that would be more than enough to buy the doll.

Now that her mum could see that she was serious, Mrs Johnson agreed to stop off at the shop after school, so Sarah could have a good look at the doll. Sarah thought that the shopkeeper was a strange old lady.

She had snowy white hair with red streaks worn in a tight bun, held in place with a long wooden clip. Her dress was completely black and nearly reached the floor.

She greeted them warmly, her smile exaggerating her crinkly eyes and dimpled pink cheeks.

"Hello my dears, how can I help you today?"

She noticed Sarah's eyes transfixed by the doll.

"Oh, is it the doll you are interested in?"

Mrs Bell reached into the window and brought out the doll.

"It comes in a very special box you know."

She handed the doll to Sarah and brought out a wooden box from under the counter.

"Here it is!"

The doll was everything Sarah had imagined and the box was a bonus. Dressed in a Victorian costume with a lace collar, the doll had a beautiful delicate face with masses of long chestnut hair. All her limbs moved easily, even her hands could be moved independently. She wore a gorgeous velvet coat with a red lining and smart black boots.

Sarah fell in love with her straight away and knew she would be hers. She would call her Victoria and would treasure her forever.

"Look at the box as well dear, it's a very special box, a magic box"

Victoria fitted in the box perfectly. It was made of a dark black wood and had lots of strange markings all over it.

Mrs Bell explained that the box had magic powers and that it was important to keep the doll inside it at night. Mrs Johnson shook her head in disbelief and asked how much the doll cost.

"I can do a special price for you, as I can see you will take care of her so well. She's a bargain at only thirty pounds."

Mrs Bell agreed to put the doll away and took a five pound deposit to secure her.

"Thank you so much mum, I'll pay you back from my earnings."

"That's OK, just make sure that you do," her Mum chided and smiled to herself.

The weeks passed and Sarah worked hard cleaning the neighbours' cars. She got lots of praise and compliments on the results and best of all, she managed to earn nearly one hundred pounds.

Then the day came, mum went with her to buy the doll. She ran into the shop and collected Victoria. Safely tucked under her arm in her special box they thanked Mrs Bell and Sarah handed over the money. They turned towards the door to go.

"Wait dear, wait a moment, don't forget to always keep her in her box at night," Mrs Bell warned.

Her usual cheery voice suddenly sounded dark and serious. But Sarah was too excited to notice.

Mrs Johnson looked perplexed." Yes of course she will."

As her mother tucked Sarah into bed that night, Victoria lay safely in her box.

Sarah was fast asleep when her younger brother Simon crept into her room. He was curious to see what was in the box.

Simon opened it gently so as not to wake his sister. When he realised it was only a doll he threw Victoria angrily across the room.

Sarah stirred slightly as he tiptoed quietly back to his room. Victoria's eyes opened wide, her eyelashes blinking wildly. She was out of the box and ready for some fun.

Winter Tales

Printed in Great Britain
by Amazon